Saphrezdako and Her Origin Story

David Lewis Hill

First Edition. Print / Paperback.

ISBN: 978-0-578-21107-7

Publisher : David Lewis Hill (self-published)

To my friends and family

Thank you for your support.

This book is my legacy to my family.

Chapter 1

Birth to Age Six

Alexander Akio Sanduregost was the son of Kira Sakura Hoskeggai and Rai Akiara Sanduregost. Kira Hoskeggai's family ran and owned Hoskeggai Light and Heavy Industries, which manufactured automobiles, aerospace parts, cutlery, and paper-based products, The headquarters for Hoskeggai Light and Heavy Industries was in Kakamigahara, Gifu Prefecture, Japan. Rai Sanduregost's family ran and owned Sanduregost Farms, the Sanduregost Restaurant chain, the Sanduregost Supermarket chain, and the Sanduregost Hotel chain, including the Sanduregost Hotel and Resort. Most of the Sanduregost family's businesses had their headquarters in Aichi Prefecture, Japan.

Kira was from Igiyama Unuma, Kakamigahara, Gifu Prefecture, Japan, and Rai was from Ichinomiya, Aichi Prefecture, Japan. Both families owned land near the Kiso River, and one day, Rai Sanduregost and Kira Hoskeggai met in a park near the river. Kira's family owned a castle in Igiyama Unuma, Kakamigahara, Gufu Prefecture, and some other land in Japan, Australia, France, Germany, Canada, and India. Rai's family owned a villa overlooking a farm that they owned in Ichinomiya, Aichi Prefecture, and some other land in Japan, Hawaii, Puerto Rico, the Philippines, Australia, and the United Kingdom. Rai's family had opened a restaurant in Kakamigahara, and one day Rai was delivering food from his family farm to the restaurant because the normal delivery person was sick that day. Kira was at the restaurant, picking up food for her family. That's how she met Rai for the second time, and after that they started to date.

Kira married Rai, and after that, lived in Kameyama, Mie Prefecture, near the Suzuka River. Rai and Kira owned and ran the Sanduregost Food Production Company, which produced tea, fruit, mandarin oranges, and cultured pearls. The headquarters for the Sanduregost Food Production Company was in Kameyama.

Kaylee Sage Quiviazanda was the daughter of Alison Savannah Borothsessa and Jaylon Caleb Quiviazanda. Alison Borothsessa's family ran and owned the Borothsessa Pharmaceutical Company, which had its headquarters in White Plains, New York. They also owned Borothsessa Plastic Fabrication Company and Borothsessa International Renewable Energy Company, which was a manufacturer and supplier of wind, solar, biomass, geothermal, biogas, and hydropower energy. Both Borothsessa International Renewable Energy Company and Borothsessa Plastic Fabrication Company had their headquarters in Mamaroneck, New York. Jaylon Quiviazanda's family owned and ran Quiviazanda Jewelry Company and Quiviazanda Fashion Retail Company, which sold eyewear, footwear, accessories, undergarments, cosmetics, and apparel. They also owned and ran Quiviazanda International Freight Company, which transported by air, road, sea, and rail. All three Quiviazanda companies had their headquarters in White Plains.

Both Alison and Jaylon were at Westchester Golf Club in Ridgeway in White Plains. Alison was coming up to a turn in the golf course, and the steering went out in her golf cart. She ran into Jaylon's golf cart, and that is how they first met.

The second time that Alison and Jaylon met was on the tennis courts in Gillie Park on Gedney Way, White Plains, New York. That day at the tennis courts, Alison was waiting for a friend who did not show, and she had to play tennis against Jaylon Quiviazanda. The third time that the Alison and Jaylon met was at the Quiviazanda Fashion Retail store in the Westchester Mall on Westchester Avenue in White Plains. Alison's girlfriend had broken her sunglasses when they were playing tennis, and Alison liked the sunglasses from Quiviazanda Fashion Retail. That's why she went there that day when Jaylon was behind the counter that day—a lot of employees were sick that day and couldn't come to work.

After the third time they met, Alison and Jaylon started dating, and a few years later, they got married. Alison and Jaylon moved to Rochelle, New York, and started the Quiviazanda Beverages Company.

Mayu Ayaka Sanduregost was the daughter of Kira and Rai Sanduregost. Maya and her brother, Alexander Akio Sanduregost, were born in Kameyama, Mie Prefecture, Japan, and went to primary and secondary school there. Mayu studied culinary arts because she wanted to be a chef. Alexander also studied culinary arts, but he did not like it that much, so he went to Kyoto University. Both Mayu and Alexander moved to Shugakuin Muromachi, Sakyo Ward, Kyoto, Kyoto Prefecture, Japan, into a wooden two-story structure with five multipurpose rooms, a living room, a dining room, and a kitchen, plus a separate storeroom from the house. (This was listed as "5LDK + S.") The driveway had a metal gate with a small walk-through door in it.

Mayu started work at Sanduregost Restaurant in Katagiharabonyama, Nishikyo Ward, Kyoto Prefecture, Japan, as a sous chef, and Alexander started as a student at Kyoto University in Sakyo Ward. Alexander also had a job while he was going to Kyoto University. He was the *patissier*, or pastry chef, at Sanduregost Restaurant in Nishinokyo Higahigekkocho, Nakagyo Ward. The Sanduregost Restaurant in Katagiharabonyama, where Mayu worked, was short on waiters one week, and Alexander was asked to help for that week.

It was during that week that Kaylee Sage Quiviazanda came in to eat with her friends from Yamadahiraocho, and while they were there, Kaylee tripped as she was going to her table. That happened to be at the same time that Alexander was walking by, and she fell into him—that was their first meeting. One day Alexander was visiting his friends in Goryominegadocho, and after he left, he went to Katsurazaka Park in Goryooeyamacho to take a walk. Kaylee Quiviazanda was doing yoga at the time, and one of her friends pushed her into Alexander as he walked past. That was the second time they met.

The third time that Kaylee and Alexander met was at Goryo Park in Kyotodaigakukatsura. Alexander was talking to some of his friends, and Kaylee passed by on her way to class at Kyoto University. She had just left her apartment, which had three multipurpose rooms, a living room, dining room, kitchen, and a storeroom (3LDK+S), in Yamadahiracho, where she also she lived with a female university friend from Japan.

The fourth time that Kaylee and Alexander met was at Kyoto University. They both had the same math class, which is when Kaylee discovered that Alexander Sanduregost was studying science and mathematics at Kyoto University, and Alexander found out that Kaylee Quiviazanda was studying chemical engineering, electrical engineering, and mechanical engineering there. Kyoto University had scheduled a trip for the engineering and science students to learn about Japanese history, buildings, and architecture.

Kaylee and Alexander were both on the same bus for the university trip. When she got up to move to a different seat to talk to some friends, the bus made a sudden stop, and Kaylee once again fell into Alexander's lap. The Kyoto University trip was to Maruyama Park, Gifu-

Kakamigahara Air and Space Museum, Nara Park, and Osaka Science Museum.

Maruyama Park is in Maruyamacho, Higahiyama Ward, Kyoto. It has bronze statues, shrines, temples, and green spaces and cherry blossoms. Alexander was walking near some cherry blossoms when some guy pushed him, and he fell onto Kaylee. Then their lips met, and they kissed.

The second stop on the trip was Gifu-Kakamigahara Air and Space Museum in Shimogiricho, which has history on aircraft, space rockets, artificial satellites, orbiters, and the aircraft industry. The third place they went to was Nara Park in Zoshicho, Nara. Kaylee was walking near a pond in and some tame deer pushed her into the water. Alexander came along and pulled her out of the pond.

The fourth place that the Kyoto University students went on their trip was to Osaka Science Museum in Nakanoshima. They saw exhibits on chemistry, science, electricity, and energy. They visited the planetarium, science gallery, and the universe and discovery exhibits. After going to the four places that were planned for the trip, they went back to Kyoto University. After that day, Alexander and Kaylee started to date.

Between the Kyoto University trip and their university gradation, both Kaylee and Alexander had ten favorite places to visit for their dates. Date one was at the Kyoto Aquarium in Kankijicho, Shimogyo Ward. It had dolphin shows, penguins, and seals. Date two was to Umekoji Park, also in Kankijicho, which had seasonal flower displays. Alexander and Kaylee's date three was to the Kyoto City Zoo in Okazaki Hoshojicho, where they saw flying squirrels, hawks, eagles, foxes, a Tsushima leopard, falcons, tigers, bears, deer, Brazilian tapirs, elephants, lions, jaguars, hyraxes, giant salamanders, gorillas, monkeys, gibbons, rhesus monkeys, red-crowned cranes, emu, peafowl, bush dogs, red pandas (also known as lesser pandas), giraffes, owls, apes, chimpanzees, Humboldt penguins, fennec foxes, meerkats, hippos, zebras, flamingoes, guinea fowl, llamas, swans, ducks, orangutans, tanukis, ostriches, sea lions, and many more animals, reptiles, and birds.

Date four was at Nijo Castle in Nijojocho, where they saw the Ninomaru Palace, Honmaru Palace, and gardens. Date five of their favorite places was Kyoto International Manga Museum in Kinpukicho. It displayed Japanese comic books and graphic novels, and had some reading areas. Alexander and Kaylee's sixth favorite place for a date was the Kyoto Botanical Garden in Shimogamo Hangicho. It had a sunken garden, water mill, a statue, and a conservatory. Date seven was an imperial palace tour in Kyotogyoen, on which they saw a park, shrines, the palace, the gardens, and a pond.

Date eight was to the Iwatayama Monkey Park, where they saw Japanese macaque monkeys, and had a boat ride from Arashiyama Tuusen. Date nine was to Arashiyama Bamboo Grove in Gearokuzancho, which had a bamboo forest and water vistas. Date ten was to Kyoto Art Center in Yamabushiyamacho. They visited both the north and south art galleries, the library, and the café.

One day Mayu was at Kyoto Art Center, trying to get creative ideas for new menu items for Sanduregost Restaurant. Kaylee Quiviazanda and Alexander Sanduregost were on a date that day, and Mayu ran into her brother—this is how she found out that Alexander was dating Kaylee.

Rai and Kira found out that their son, Alexander, was dating Kaylee when they visited him at Kyoto University and saw him talking to her in Goryo Park, one of their meeting places. One of Alexander's friends told his parents that he was at a park near Kyoto University, but his friend did not tell them why he was there, and that was how Kaylee met his parents.

Alison and Jaylon met Alexander when they went to Kyoto University to sell beverages from Quiviazanda Beverages Company. That was how they found out that Kaylee was dating Alexander.

When Kaylee and Alexander graduated from Kyoto University, they both moved to New York and got married. They lived with Alison Borothsessa and Jaylon Quiviazanda in Westchester, New York, for about a year, after which they found a house in Manhattan on the Upper East Side.

Kaylee worked at John F. Kennedy International Airport, which originally was called Idlewild Airport, as an aircraft mechanic. The airport was located in Queens, New York. Alexander worked for Lyeor Multigrid Company, a multinational electricity and gas utility company that served New York State. His office was located in Brooklyn, where he worked as an accounting director for the company.

Sora Mya Sanduregost was the daughter of Kaylee and Alexander. Sora was born at New York-Presbyterian Hospital (originally called New York Hospital) on East Sixty-Eighth Street in Manhattan.

At age three, Sora attended an international preschool on Manhattan's Upper East Side, located on East Eighty-Sixth Street. At age four, Sora left preschool to attend a language school in Chelsea on West Twenty-Ninth Street. The school offered Japanese language classes and programs for ages four to sixteen. Sora Sanduregost went to kindergarten at age five at a school on Riverside Boulevard on New York's Upper West Side, finishing kindergarten at age six.

Chapter2

Age Seven to Age Eighteen

Sora Sanduregost started first grade at age six at a Manhattan public school on East Sixty-Seventh Street on the Upper East Side. The school taught students from first grade to eighth grade. One day she when to the New York Public Library on East Sixty-Seventh Street to do research for her Latin class. Sora was learning to speak and write Latin at age seven. Then, when she was reading comics, graphic novels, and nonfiction books on science, social sciences, health, and mind and body at a reading table, a young boy came over and sat across from her. They started to talk about different things and became best friends. Sora was age seven, and her new friend, Zack Faoughkal, was eight.

During the summer when Sora was eight, she went to visited Rai and Kira in Kameyama, Japan, located near the Suzuka River, and she learned about breathing meditation that can overcome stress and help to find balance. Sora also learned asana postures called Padmasana (or lotus pose), seiza, Hankafuza (half-lotus), and Kekkafuza (full lotus), with and without using a round cushion (called a *zafu*) and a typical kapok-filled zabuton.

Kira and Rai taught Sora meditation and basic *ki*, also known as chi, and afterward, they gave Sora a nickname *Saphronia*, which means wise; she also used saffron with fish a lot. When Saphronia was in Japan, she also learned more Japanese, and when she got back to New York, she took classes at the Japanese Cultural Center in Midtown Manhattan. Also, when Sora returned to New York that summer, her mother, Kaylee, gave her the nickname *Sophrona*, but Sora made that nickname shorter and turned it into Sophia.

When Sora was nine years old and in the third grade, Alexander taught her and Kaylee a traditional Japanese martial art called Hojojutsu. Also when Sora was nine, she started reading books about music theory and martial arts theory at the library. She learned about the musical alphabet, scales, intervals, chords, and key signatures from the music theory book, and the book on martial arts theory talked about the definition and conception of a battle or fight, strategy, tactics, technique, method of training, and assimilation. The book also had stretching techniques for martial arts, such as dynamic stretching, active stretching, passive stretching, and isometric stretching.

Sora finally became old enough, at age ten, for other martial arts, which Alexander then began to teach her. The Japanese martial arts he taught was aikido and jujitsu.

Also when Sora was ten, and she started in the fourth-grade band, playing the drums. She met a new friend named Anna Rayathsam, who plays the flute (also known as the western concert flute). Both Anna and Sora had the same fourth-grade music theory class, and they learned about musical notation, expression, form or structure, harmony, chords, melody, rhythm, consonance and dissonance, scales and modes, pitch or tone, tuning, intervals, counterpoint, durational proportions, composition, orchestration, and ornamentation.

Anna gave Sora another nickname one day—Inez. Anna said that Inez meant *pure*. Anna and Sora liked to hang out at Saint Catherine's Park on First Avenue between East Sixty-Seventh and East Sixty-Eighth Streets on the Upper East Side.

One day after school, Anna's mother, Ivy, took Anna and Sora to Washington Square Park in Greenwich Village. Ivy played a portable digital piano, without the use of a keyboard amplifier or loud speaker; Sora played a drum set; and Anna played the western concert flute. The three played in Washington Square Park for two hours. Zack Faoughkal and his dad, Christopher, came by to see them play.

Little did Sora Sanduregost know that she could channel enthusiastic, magical energy through the drumsticks and enchant most audiences that listened to her play. This magical only affected about thirty people, and it had to be unamplified and not transmitted electronically. When Sora was age eleven and in fifth grade, she started to play violin. Her friend Anna learned to play piano. They both played in the fifth-grade band at that time. One day during spring, Sora, Anna, and Ivy had an audition for

Music Under New York (MUNY), and all three of them passed.

That fall, Sora, Anna, and Ivy performed in the New York City subway—Sora played violin, Anna played digital stage piano, and Ivy played viola. Little did Sora know that, as with her drumsticks, she could channel happy, magical energy through her violin bow and enchant audiences. Again, the happy magical energy that she made affected about thirty people, and it had to be unamplified and not transmitted by digital means.

That day when Sora performed in the subway, the passengers who went to and from the trains in the subway were in a happy mood because of her enchanting and magical music.

About a year later, when Sora turned age twelve, she started gymnastics with Anna. They went to Gaudonogard Educational Institute on York Avenue in Manhattan. Gaudonogard Educational Institute had programs and classes for cooking, Tae Kwon Do, gymnastics, kids CrossFit, and skateboarding. Sora took a cooking class, Tae Kwon Do, and gymnastics for one year at Gaudonogard. During that year in her gymnastics class, Sora studied and learned elementary gymnastics, artistic gymnastics, and freestyle gymnastics. Anna took skateboarding, cooking, and kids' CrossFit classes at Gaudonogard.

Anna's first boyfriend was Peregrino Bregareld. She met him while she was skateboarding one day, and they dated for about three months. Around the third month that Anna and Peregrino were dating, a new girl started to skateboard at Gaudonogard; her name was Neka Danveraugh. Peregrino and Neka bonded over sports and skiing. Once Neka Danveraugh, the sports girl, and Peregrino Bregareld, the skateboarder, bonded, he stopped dating Anna; Anna didn't know how to ski.

Anna lost the guy to the sports girl, Neka, because Anna was a more creative girl than sporty. Both Sora t and Anna took the cooking class because they liked being creative.

When she was around age thirteen, Sora had nine weeks of karate classes at a karate school in Manhattan.

At age fourteen, when they were in eight grade, both Sora and Anna had mixed martial arts classes at Marjiliathar Mixed Martial Arts, a self-defense and martial arts school on Broadway on the Upper West Side in Manhattan. Sora and Anna learned Brazilian jujitsu, kickboxing, Tae Kwon Do, Krav Maga, Mauy Thai, and Kaju Bujutsu Kwai.

During Anna's first week at Marjiliathar, she started dating Liam Thruendage, who had started class with her; both of them were fourteen. Anna dated Liam for one year, but she stopped dating him when she started high school. Liam and Anna drifted apart because they attended different schools after Liam and his family moved away from Manhattan.

Sora and Anna started ninth grade at a Manhattan public high school, located on East Seventy-Sixth Street on the Upper East Side. Sora Sanduregost's classes that year were global literature, Spanish, physical education, geometry, foundations of mathematics, and global studies.

Anna's ninth-grade classes were global literature, French, physical education, foundations of mathematics, global studies, and geometry.

Both Sora and Anna were in the same classes for global literature and physical education. During that same year, when Sora was fifteen, she started ballet at the Upper East Side Dance Center on Lexington Avenue on Manhattan's Upper East Side.

Sora's tenth-grade classes the following year of high school were global literature, physical education, chemistry, algebra, trigonometry and computational thinking, global studies, and beginning guitar. Anna's classes in tenth grade were global literature, Spanish, physical education, algebra, trigonometry and computational thinking, global studies, and visual arts. Both Sora and Anna had the same classes for global literature, algebra, trigonometry and computational thinking, and global studies. They also had the same classes for jazz dance and modern dance at the Upper East Side Dance Center.

At age sixteen, Sora and Anna started to have boyfriends, and they were both dating, although Anna was on her third boyfriend when Sora had her first boyfriend.

Sora was dating Zack Faoughkal, and Anna was dating Hayden Tanoughril. Zack and Hayden were best friends.

Anna first met Hayden when his best friend, Zack, and he started classes for jazz dance and modern dance at the Upper East Side Dance Center. The boys were seventeen at the time. Hayden was known for being creative, and he also was a musician like Anna, Ivy, and Sora.

The following year, Sora's eleventh-grade classes in high school were American literature, yoga and barre, physics, precalculus, US history, and guitar. Anna's classes that year were American literature, lifetime fitness, precalculus, physics, US history, and ceramics.

Sora and Anna had the same classes for was American literature and US history. During the summer she was seventeen, Sora, also known as Saphronia, went to Japan to visit Hiroyuki Ren Hoskeggai, her mother's brother who lived in Osaka Prefecture. He owned and ran Hoskeggai Martial Arts Center in Osakajo, Chuo Ward, Osaka. Also, Hiroyuki lived in a house with his wife in Kitahama, Chuo Ward. His wife's name was Akira Kuri Hoskeggai, and she owned a Japanese chestnut farm that was located between Osaka City and Nara City.

Saphronia was in Japan for two months, and during that time she when to Hoskeggai Martial Arts Center to learn about aikido, judo, Taido, karate, gymnastics, and jujitsu. Also, Saphronia went to Akira's Japanese chestnut farm to get some chestnuts to make a traditional Japanese dessert called *shibukawani*.

When Anna and Sora turned age seventeen, they both got part-time jobs. Anna started working at a local café on the Upper East Side; Sora started working at her mom's work as an aircraft painter. During the weekends, Sora would ride with her mother to work, and during the week, a friend of the family would take Sora to work after school.

The café where Anna worked was within walking distance of school and home; she did not have to ride with anyone, but sometimes friends would walk with her.

The classes that Sora, also known as Saphronia, took in twelfth grade were English, yoga and Zumba, audio science, calculus, economics and finance, participation in government, and public speaking. Anna's classes that year were English, yoga and Zumba, calculus, art and environment, economics and finance, participation in government, and public speaking.

Sora and Anna had the same classes for English, yoga and Zumba, economics and finance, participation in government, and public speaking.

The high school had a weight room, and one day when no one was in the room, Sora start lifting with 135 (2x45+bar), 225 (4x45+bar), 315 (6x45+bar), 405 (8x45+bar), 495 (10x45+bar), 585 (12x45+bar), and finally 675 (14x45+bar) pounds, and she used all the forty-five–pound weights that were in the weight room at the time and used a seven-foot barbell with a maximum load capacity of a thousand pounds, and the barbell weight was forty-five pounds.

Sora didn't know that her genetics were different from other humans because she was half elf and a DNA–TNA human. Also, Sora could lift five times her own weight over her head or lift from the ground. The weight for lifting a heavy load or lifting over her head was 680 pounds, and lifting off the ground was 1,360 pounds; this was because of her different genetic code.

At the end of the school year, both Sora (also known as Saphronia, Inez, and Dakota) and Anna graduated from high school at the age of eighteen.

Anna and Sora were in the subway the next day after graduation, and they met a female musician named Violet Brybanenth, who was playing a bass guitar. They talked to her after she got done playing for the day and found out that she too was part of the Music Under New York (MUNY). They talked about making a local rock band.

They formed the rock band about a week later. For their rock band, Sora played guitar and sang lead vocals, Anna played piano or keyboard and was a backup singer, Hayden Tanoughril played drums, and Violet Brybanenth played bass guitar and was a backup singer.

Violet came up the band name SHAV, but Sora thought it was not distinct enough, so Sora came up with

Sabilbonie or Annathirionne, and the band voted for Annathirionne.

The band Annathirionne played at local cafés and at some local restaurants in New York. They were not old enough to play at bars, so they played at other venues, but that was OK with them. One of the venues where Annathirionne played was the café were Anna worked.

Chapter 3

Ages Nineteen to Twenty

The café where Annathirionne played was in Greenwich Village on MacDougal Street. Sora Sanduregost was nineteen at the time.

Sora quit the job as an aircraft painter and started a job as a part-time janitor at a science research complex on Saint Nicholas Terrace in Harlem. She worked evenings as a janitor, and during the day she played in her rock band. Her evening work hours were from five to eight o'clock. Anna continued working at the café. Her work hours were the same as Sora's—from five to eight o'clock in the evening.

Annathirionne was together as a rock band for about a year and a half but then took a temporary hiatus. Sora started working nights (9:00–11:45) at the science research complex as a janitor in the science lab wing and the arachnid lab wing at the age of twenty.

After Annathirionne when on hiatus, Veraughqua Aerospace had a singing contest to select a space tourist to go up to the Veraughqua commercial space station. Sora applied for the singing competition and got in. Sora worked at night and went to the competitions during the evenings.

One day when Sora was working, she heard the spiders say they were hungry. Sora kept a drink with her that had amino acids and protein, and just before the spiders started talking to her, she had spilled some waste liquid into her drink. The waste that was spilled was telomerase, guanosine, glycosylase, graphene nanoparticles, spherical fullerenes, and cylindrical fullerenes.

After that, Sora said to the spiders in the arachnid lab, "I am not the one who feeds you," and the spiders could understand what she said.

About a month later, Sora learned she was among the top five in the singing competition, and the top five would go up to Veraughqua commercial space station in a crew capsule spacecraft that could hold seven crew members. The Veraughqua commercial space station conducted experiments in biology, physics, meteorology, and space tourism. Module configuration for the Veraughqua commercial space station started from the main module. The main module had docking port at one end and a service module at the other end. The physics module, biology module, meteorology module, and space tourist and food garden module were on the main module. The physics module had four empty berthing ports and an airlock at one end. The other end was connected to the main module. The biology module had four empty berthing ports and an airlock at one end, and the other end was connected to the main module. The meteorology module had four empty berthing ports and an airlock at one end, and the other end was connected to the main module. The space tourist and food garden module had three empty berthing ports and an airlock at one end, and the other end was connected to the main module. Also, the space tourist module had a short external truss that space tourists could hold on to; the truss was in the place where a berthing port would be. The service module had the main module connected at one end, and the other end had external trusses that had a solar array attached to it. The trusses also held a heat radiator, and the side of the module had two berthing ports. The top five singers who won the Veraughqua singing contest would be on the Veraughqua commercial space station for seven days and then come back to Earth. During one of the days that week, the space station had problems in its space weather phenomena–detection software, as well as connection problems with communications to Earth and other satellites. Also, Veraughqua was having software problems on the ground during that week after the space tourists went up to the space station.

During each day, a space tourist would go out and do a space walk, with a tether to the space tourist module and the small truss for tourists. On day one at the space station, no tourists went on a space walk. On day two, Gretchen Nysageskel went on a space walk. She was from Buffalo, New York. On day three, Kevin Snollshther went on a space walk; he was also from Buffalo, New York. On day four, Alice Chruphskel went on a space walk; she was from San Francisco, California. On day five, Wade Scheghshroth went on a space walk; he was from Los

Angeles. On day six, Sora Sanduregost went on a space walk; she was from Manhattan. On day seven, no tourists went on a space walk.

On day six, when the four space tourists and part of the top-five singers from the Veraughqua singing contest were in the space station, and Sora Sanduregost was on a space walk, a high-speed stream of solar wind hit Sora and missed the space station. Sora got hit with both solar wind and higher levels of space radiation, which made alterations, or mutations, to her genetics. The high-speed stream of solar wind and higher levels of space radiation changed her dormant ancient-century and millennium half-elf DNA. Also, Sora's half-elf and hybrid DNA–TNA (deoxyribonucleic acid–threose nucleic acid) genetic ancestors had come from a different world or planet, but she didn't know that she was half elf or that she had natural-hybrid DNA–TNA genetics—or that she had a magical bloodline.

The mishap in outer space caused Sora to be stronger and more magical than before because of the elf DNA, human TNA, and the waste liquid from the science research complex, combined with space radiation and solar wind. Sora Sanduregost now could live to age 300 to 450 because her elf DNA was turned on for age.

Also, her body had a unknown defense mechanism in her TNA that made her withstand extreme temperatures and high energy. This defense mechanism was there before she got hit with the solar wind and radiation. The defense mechanism protected and prevented her from being killed by extreme temperature and high energy. If the extreme temperature or energy was high enough, she would pass out, or her body would go into hibernation. When they were at extreme levels, however, they could make alterations or mutations in her genetics.

After Sora came back from the Veraughqua commercial space station, she started an art project for Anna Rayathsam and Gretchen Nysageskel. When she was at Leesville junkyard in Rahway, New Jersey, looking around for metal and other stuff to make an art piece, she got a phone call from her parents, telling her that her fiancé, Zack Faoughkal, whom she was soon to marry, was dead. Zack had been killed by a robber at a gas station when she was up in space.

Sora was so upset that she flipped over a car in the junkyard and found that she had extraordinary strength. A little after that, she had the idea to be an abnormal hero, and she came up with a hero name by combining Saphronia,

Inez, and Dakota—using *Saphr* from Saphronia, *ez* from Inez, and *dako* from Dakota to make up the hero name Saphrezdako. The combination of the names to make *Saphrezdako* meant "wise, pure, friend, ally."

After that, Sora's house was robbed. Just as the robber was running out, Sora shot magic ice balls at him and hit him, but he kept running. She also hit his car, not with an ice ball but with a white plasma chain spell that looked like snowflakes forming a chain. It hit the trunk of his car, and that, the robber gave back all the stuff he had taken; he sent it back by mail.

Chapter 4:

Age Twenty-One to Age Twenty-Seven

When Sora Sanduregost, also known as Saphrezdako, turned twenty-one, she left the janitor job at the science research complex in Harlem, and her best friend, Anna Rayathsam, left her job at the café on the Upper East Side of Manhattan. That same year, both Sora and Anna moved in to Inaskelshy Apartments; the building was on Sixth Avenue between West Tenth Street and Eleventh Street in Greenwich Village. Inaskelshy Apartments had six floors and thirty-four apartments.

Sora and Anna share an apartment on the second floor that had a half bath and full bath, kitchen, living room with three windows and a wood-burning fireplace, and two bedrooms—one had two windows, and the other bedroom had only one window. Anna took the larger bedroom with two windows so she could have a fashion-design work area, and Sora took the smaller bedroom with one window because she did not need a lot of space. She let Anna have the larger room because Anna would start fashion school soon.

Once Anna and Sora got settled into their apartment, they both started college at Greenwich Village

College on Fifth Avenue, between Sixth Avenue and University Place, in Greenwich Village, Lower Manhattan. Greenwich Village College had associates degrees in fashion design, fashion marketing, graphics design, interior design, liberal arts, business, health administration, information systems management, and accounting. The college also had bachelor's degree programs in applied general studies, humanities, social sciences, applied data analytics and visualization, health care management, information systems management, leadership and management studies, marketing estates, real estate, hotel and tourism management, sports management, architectural design, communication design, fashion design, fine arts, illustration, integrated design, photography, product design, strategic design and management, urban design, and financial services.

One rainy day when Sora was twenty-one, her friend Anna had left some fashion-design books on the living room table, and Sora started to read them. After that, Sora started to design her own custom-made evening dress.

Both Anna and Sora got new jobs at the age of twenty-two. Sora Sanduregost started working at the Greenwich Village Police Station as a janitor. The police station was on Tenth Street. Anna started working in a café that was in Tasperqua Bookstore, which was on East Seventeenth Street, Union Square, Midtown Manhattan.

Sora, known as Saphrezdako, finished her custom-made evening dress. It has a column silhouette that was calf-length, or tea length. It had a scoop neck, shaped like the letter U. The column-silhouette dress was made of stealth dyes with multiwall nanotubes, para-aramid fibers, and meta-aramid fibers. The three zippers on the dress were made of carbon fiber. The one zipper on the back went from the neck to the hips, and the other two zippers—one on the left side and one on the right—went from her thighs to the hem of the dress.

Sora also made custom-made panties to go with the dress. The style was hipster, and they were made of heat-resistant silk, para-aramid fibers, and a meta-aramid fiber blend; her bra was made of the same thing. The custom-made evening dress and undergarments could withstand 500 Celsius or 930 Fahrenheit.

In that same year, a new restaurant, Sanduregost Restaurant, opened in Union Square in Midtown Manhattan.

One night, Sora Sanduregost was wearing her custom-made evening dress when she went to Sanduregost Restaurant for a evening meal. When she finished, she started walking home along East Fourteenth Street, and on her way, she passed through an area that did not have any security cameras. On the corner of East Fourteenth Street and Union Square West, a guy in a black hooded sweatshirt started to attack her. She dodged his knife and grabbed his arm and flipped him. After that a guy in a red hooded sweatshirt with a handgun shot at Sora. It hit her custom-made evening dress, and the dress stopped all five bullets that he had fired—the para-aramid fiber could withstand knifes and bullets.

Then Sora made her way to the red hooded guy and kicked the gun down to the ground. She flipped the guy in the red hood with a twist that broke his arm. After that, Sora somehow healed his arm without her knowing that she was healing him. He was in so much pain from the healing process that he passed out. With both guys on the ground, Sora walked home.

After that night, Sora had the idea to make a blue custom-made evening dress for Anna. She made the dress of para-aramid fibers and meta-aramid fibers that could withstand 500 Celsius. The zippers were made of carbon fiber with blue dye mixed in. This time, though, she made the dress without the stealth dyes. She also made blue custom-made hipster panties made of heat-resistant silk, para-aramid fibers, and a meta-aramid fibers blend, also made to withstand 500 Celsius; the bra was made of the same thing and same color.

When Sora gave the evening dress and undergarments to Anna, she said she liked the bra and dress, but did not like the hipster-style panties, so she asked Sora to make custom-made bikini-style panties, and she did. Sora kept the blue custom-made hipster-style panties for herself, and made an extra blue custom-made bra to go with it.

At the age of twenty-three, both Anna and Sora graduated with associate's degrees from Greenwich Village College. Anna's degree was in fashion design; Sora's degree was in liberal arts.

One day at Sora and Anna's apartment, Anna was cooking food. She needed to take the food out of the oven, but all her pot holders were in the wash. She went to the living room and grabbed her blue custom-made bra and panties from living room table and used them as pot holders. When

Sora came home then. She came into the kitchen and saw Anna holding the pot with her custom-made bra and panties. Sora laughed and then said, "Looks like you found a new use for your underwear. It's a good thing that can withstand oven temperatures because they're made of aramid fibers."

Anna laughed and said, "Yeah, it's a good thing."

When Sora was twenty-four, she went for a bachelor's degree at Greenwich Village College. Anna started working at a new job that same year as a fashion designer at Sweradaugha Fashion Company. The company was on Greene Street in SoHo, Lower Manhattan.

In her college classes, Sora learned the Pangasinan, Kapampangan, Ilocano, Tagalog, and Filipino languages. Also during that same year, Sora designed a battle dress and some armor to go with it.

At the age of twenty-five, during one of Sora's college breaks, she went to visit family in the Philippines. Sora went to JFK Airport and got on a Hoskeggai private business jet. She landed at Mabalacat International Airport in the Philippines. One of her guy cousins from the Sanduregost family was waiting for her with a car that was rented just for her to use while she was there.

Sora and her cousin left Mabalacat, Pampanga, Philippines, to visit other cousins in Agoo, La Union. Sora's cousins ran Sanduregost Supermarket in Agoo. Her cousins in Agoo were Filipino of Japanese descent.

One day in Agoo, a local rock band from Tarlac City asked her to play music with them because one of their band members got sick. They needed someone to fill in because the band would be playing in Tarlac City. The Tarlac City rock band and Sora left Agoo for Tarlac City in a van.

The rock band and Sora stayed at a hotel on Manila N Road, also known as R-9, in Tarlac City. They went to Maria Cristina Park and played music, and after the performance, the band headed back to the hotel.

Sora decided to walk to a restaurant that was on the corner of Romulo Boulevard and Champaca Street. She was wearing her custom-made evening dress at the time. Suddenly, three guys tried to attack her. The first guy came from behind her, but she grabbed him and flipped him into the bushes. The second guy had a rope with him, and he tried to tie her up, but she used Hojojutsu to restrain him with the rope he had. The third guy got in his car and tried to run her over, but she stopped the car and threw the car— with him in it—up in a nearby tree.

Then he found a gun in the car and start shooting at her; it hit her dress. She threw an ice ball at the gun and hit it. The gun and the ice ball hit the roof of the car. The car lost its balance in the tree and fell to the ground.

The guy inside was still alive. He jumped out, saying, "What just happened?" He ran off after that.

Sora went into the restaurant and had her meal. On her way back hotel, as she was walking on the same road, two of the guys who had tried to attack her were still lying in the same place that she'd left them. She went over to the guy she'd tied up in rope and untied him. Sora had him get into the back seat of the car.

The guy who already was in the car said, "What are you doing?"

Sora said, "Would friends or family believe that you hit a woman with a car and made this much damage to the car?" She picked up the car with the two guys in it and made it look like the car hit the tree instead of her. Sora said, "Now call your friends or family to help you get home."

"Wait," one guy said, "What's your name?"

"My nickname is Saphrezdako."

The two guys finally called someone for help, but they did not tell anyone about Sora. They just went home.

Sora went back to the hotel to sleep, and the next day, the band took Sora back to Agoo. She said her goodbyes to her cousins, and then she when to Mabalacat International Airport to again get on her family's private jet, this time headed back to New York and home to her apartment.

About a week later, the two guys who had attacked her were in a bar, getting drunk and telling the story about her.

Someone in the bar said, "You guys tell good stories when you get drunk."

Then the two guys left the bar and went home.

At the age of twenty-six, Sora learned Romance languages at Greenwich Village College; her classes were Spanish, Portuguese, and French.

At the age of twenty-seven, Sora Mya Sanduregost, also known as Saphrezdako, earned a bachelor's degree in leadership and management studies.

In the same year, Sora finished her battle dress and armor, which was similar to her custom-made evening dress. The custom-made battle dress was a column silhouette that was knee-length with a scoop neck. The dress was made of black stealth dyes, para-aramid fibers, meta-aramid fibers, and carbon nanotubes fiber. The three zippers were made of carbon nanotubes fiber. The zipper on the back went from the neck to just above the hips, and the other two zippers—one on the left and the other on the right—went from her hips to the hem of the dress. As she had with her evening dress, she also she made custom-made panties to go with the dress, though these were in a boy-shorts style. They were made of para-aramid fiber, meta-aramid fiber, and carbon nanotubes fiber blend; her bra was made of the same thing.

The armor was knee pads and elbow pads made of para-aramid fiber, meta-aramid fiber, titanium fiber, and carbon nanotubes fiber with titanium caps. Also, she made gloves to go with the knee pads and elbow pads, and they were made of para-aramid fiber and meta-aramid fiber.

Her evening dress had been made to withstand 500 degrees Celsius, or 930 degrees Fahrenheit, but this battle dress was made to withstand 1,600 degrees Celsius, or 2,912 degrees Fahrenheit.

Sora thought that she might have future ideas for a third dress, although she hadn't come up with anything yet.

At this time, Sora also started work as a business analyst in marketing and advertising for Sweradaugha Fashion Company. During Anna's college years, she would bring home books about fashion design and the fashion industry, and Sora would read them. Now she could put that information to good use, along with her degree in liberal arts and degree in leadership and management studies.

Now both Anna and Sora worked at Sweradaugha Fashion Company in SoHo, and they still had the same apartment on the second floor of Inaskelshy Apartments on Sixth Avenue in Greenwich Village.

Character list for Saphrezdako (book 1)

(JATL)

* * * Birth name * * *

Sora Mya Sanduregost

(She is Saphrezdako.)

* * * Nicknames * * *

Saphronia (means "wise")

Sophrona (means "wise")

Sophia (means "wisdom")

Inez (means "pure")

Dakota (means "friend, ally, forever smiling")

Sophia Dakota

(means "wisdom, friend, ally, forever smiling")

Saphrezdako (Saphronia + Inez + Dakota)
(means "wise, pure, friend, ally")

Sophia Mya Sanduregost

* * * * * * * * * * * * * * * * *

Kaylee Sage Sanduregost
(Sora's mom; lives in and is from the US)

Kaylee Sage Quiviazanda
(Sora's mom's maiden name)

Alison Savannah Borothsessa
(Sora's mom's mom's maiden name; lives in
and is from US)

Jaylon Caleb Quiviazanda
(Sora's mom's dad; lives in and is from US)

Alexander Akio Sanduregost

(Sora's dad; lives in US; from Japan)

Rai Akiara Sanduregost

(Sora's dad's dad; lives in and is from Japan)

Kira Sakura Hoskeggai

(Sora's dad's mom's maiden name; lives in and is from Japan)

Mayu Ayaka Sanduregost

(Alexander Sanduregost's sister; lives in and is from Japan)

Hiroyuki Ren Hoskeggai

(Kira Hoskeggai's brother; lives in and is from Japan)

Akira Kuri Hoskeggai

(Hiroyuki Hoskeggai's wife; lives in and is from Japan)

Zack Faoughkal

(friend at the local library)

Christopher Faoughkal

(Zack's dad)

Anna Ivorine Rayathsam
(Sora's friend since fourth grade)

Ivy Rayathsam
(Anna's mother)

Peregrino Bregareld
(Anna's first boyfriend)

Neka Danveraugh
(Sports girl)

Liam Thruendage
(Anna's second boyfriend)

Hayden Orion Tanoughril
(Anna's third boyfriend)

Violet Dana Brybanenth
(bass player)

Gretchen Nysageskel
(from Buffalo, New York; female space tourist)

Kevin Snollshther

(from Buffalo, New York; male space tourist)

Alice Chruphskel

(from San Francisco, California; female space tourist)

Wade Scheghshroth

(from Los Angeles, California; male space tourist)

* * * * * * * * * * * * * * * * *

Last names, nicknames, and related elements are trademarks of David Hill.

Lift Weight and Lifespan

Dwarf - Can lift 7x their own weight - Life span 266 to 400 years

Millennium Elf - Can lift 7x their own weight - Life span 6658 to 9988 years

Century Elf - Can lift 6x their own weight - Life span 665 to 998 years

Millennium Half-elf - Can lift 5x their own weight - Life span 3000 to 4500 years

Century Half-elf - Can lift 4x their own weight - Life span 300 to 450 years

(DNA-TNA) Human - Can lift 5x their own weight - Life span 125 to 290 years

(TNA) Human - Can lift 4x their own weight - Life span 300 to 332 years

(DNA) Human - Can lift 3x their own weight - Life span 83 to 125 years

Sora's Abilities

Birth name: Sora Mya Sanduregost

Nicknames: Saphronia, Sophrona, Sophia, Inez, Dakota, Saphrezdako

(JATL—Japanese-American Timeline)

* * * * * * * * * * * * * *
Skills, Powers, and Abilities
* * * * * * * * * * * * * *
Musician

Musically talented

Guitarist

Singer

Gymnastics

Dancing

Stanford-Binet IQ 138 (gifted or very superior intelligence)

Engineer

Metalworking ability

Metalsmith

Blacksmith

Machinist

Swordsmith

Bladesmith

Woodworker

Leatherworker

Mixed martial arts

Bojutsu

Aikido

Bujutsu

Enshin kaikan

Hojojutsu

Itto-ryu

Karate

Kendo

Kenjutsu

Kobudo

Kyudo

Kokondo

Shorinji kempo

Taido

Yabusame

Yoseikan budo

Jujitsu

Boxing

Judo

Multiple martial arts ability

Multiple language ability

Multiple writing systems ability

Note: She is part DNA–TNA human, elf (hereditary), witch (hereditary), sorcerer, and some changes from outer space radiation and solar wind

Regenerative healing factor

Enhanced immune system

Thermal resistance

Energy resistance

Large jump ability

Enhanced flexibility

Enhanced dexterity

Enhanced swordsmanship

Enhanced crafting

Enhanced craftsmanship/forging/metalworking/smithing

Enhanced combat

Supernatural strength

Supernatural speed

Supernatural stamina

Supernatural durability

Supernatural agility

Supernatural reflexes

Supernatural leap

Animal telepathy

Zoopathy

Teleportation

Spatial awareness

Levitation

Alchemy

Spell casting

Hand blasts

Ball projection

Bolt projection

Air-beam emission

Panmnesia

Barrier magic

Force-field magic

Crystal magic

Elemental magic

Elemental spike projection

Elemental combat

Arachnid manipulation

Reptile manipulation

Empathic voice (vocal pathokinesis)

Music manipulation (symphokinesis)

Telekinetic teleportation—teleport with the use of telekinesis

Telekinesis—using the mind to influence/manipulate/move matter/objects

Magic manipulation and generation

Sphere manipulation and generation (sfaírakinesis)

Chain manipulation and generation (alysídakinesis)

Elemental manipulation

Air manipulation and generation (aerokinesis)

Wind manipulation and generation (aerokinesis)

Oxygen manipulation and generation (oxikinesis)

Earth manipulation and generation (geokinesis)

Stone manipulation

Fire manipulation and generation (pyrokinesis)

Blue-fire manipulation and generation (azur-pyrokinesis)

Heat manipulation and generation (calokinesis/pyrokinesis)

Plasma manipulation and generation (plasmakinesis)

Electric-fire manipulation and generation (electro-pyrokinesis)

Scald manipulation and generation

Moisture manipulation

Water manipulation and generation (hydrokinesis)

Hydroportation—teleport via water and water sources

Water that carries an electric current (hydro-electrokinesis)

Electricity manipulation and generation (electrokinesis)

Spark manipulation and generation (scintillakinesis)

Electrical ice manipulation and generation (cyro-electrokinesis)

Chi manipulation (tsikinesis)

Cold manipulation and generation (cryokinesis)

Ice manipulation and generation (cryokinesis)

Elemental generation

* *

Note: some additional skills and abilities can be learned from books or scrolls.

* *

Before outer space

* Light load: 266 pounds

* Medium load: 266–453 pounds

* Heavy load: 453–680 pounds

* Lift over head: 680 pounds

* Lift off ground: 1,360 pounds

* Push or drag: 3,400

* 4,351 pounds for pass-out point

After outer space (without the use of magic)

* Light load: 27,200 pounds or 13.6 US tons

* Medium load: 27,200–54,400 pounds

* Heavy load: 54,400–81,600 pounds

* Lift over head: 81,600 pounds or 40.8 US tons

* Lift off ground: 204,000 pounds or 102 US tons

* Push or drag: 408,000 pounds or 204 US tons

* Pass-out point: 522,136 pounds or 261.068 US tons

* Breaking or crush point: 1,972,513 pounds or 986.2565 US tons

* *

Sora's maximum temperature that she can withstand is between 29,727 and 2,000,000 degrees Celsius.

About the Author

David Lewis Hill writes fiction books on a variety of topics and in various genres. He thinks writing a book is the best way to leave a legacy behind that can benefit family members, as well as benefiting the world and friends. Stories and book series can last more than a generation and can make a good legacy. His family built their house from the foundation to the roof, and they left that as their legacy. David had the idea to start writing stories and books as a legacy to his family and to future generations.

When David was younger he did a lot of traveling with his parents, and he also took a lot of pictures during his travels, which helped to develop his interest in photography. He has made his photos available for public viewing. Some of his book covers use his photos, which he took with his digital camera. Other book covers use fractal images generated by his computer. He also has a vast collection of music on CD and vinyl and has a wide range of musical tastes.

David is known to be affectionate yet shy at times and likes to keep most things private, if he can. He can be open about things when asked, but questions must be within reason or within his morals, which are expressed in his noble character. He is also compassionate, gentle, and merciful to a point.